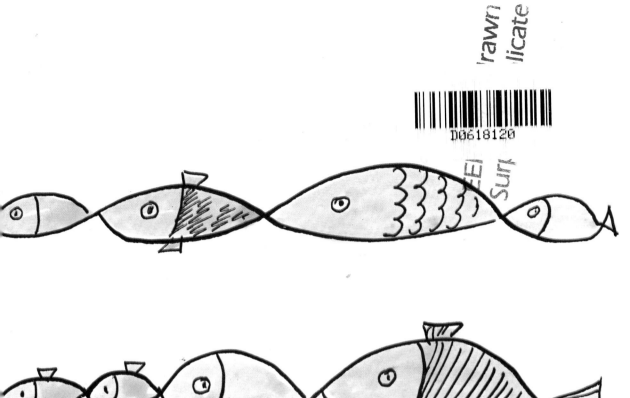

GERTIE & GUS

written and illustrated by

LISL WEIL

PARENTS' MAGAZINE PRESS

NEW YORK

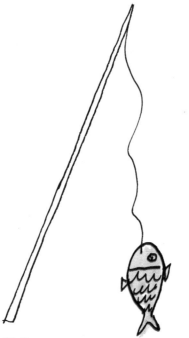

10 9 8 7 6 5 4 3 2 1
Library of Congress Cataloging in Publication Data
Weil, Lisl.
Gertie and Gus.
    SUMMARY: The ambitious wife of a bear who loves to fish changes
their comfortable and simple home life by pushing her
husband into bigger and bigger business endeavors.
They both learn something from the experience.
    [1. Fishing—Fiction.   2. Bears—Fiction]
I. Title
PZ7.W433Ge [E]   77-4757
ISBN 0-8193-0911-7
ISBN 0-8193-0912-5 lib. bdg.

GERTIE and GUS

GUS loved fishing. He was good at it, too.

Every morning Gus took his old fishing rod
and went down to the sea to fish.

Every afternoon Gus brought home a fine fish,
and Gertie would cook it for dinner.

How Gus loved his fish dinners!

Then one day Gus came home with an extra fine fish, and Gertie served only plain potatoes. No fish!

Gus got just plain potatoes three nights in a row!
Then he saw what was happening.
"I've been selling your fish for a good
price," Gertie said happily.
"And with the money
I bought you a surprise."
It was a big handsome net for catching lots of fish.
"The change will do you good," explained Gertie.
"We'll always have our own fish for dinner. And I can sell
the rest."
"All right," said good-natured Gus.

It was true.
With his new fishing net,
Gus easily caught many fish.

Every day he brought back a bucketful.
And every day he and Gertie
ate a fine fish dinner.

Of course, Gertie was so busy selling the rest
of the catch that, often, Gus had to cook their dinner.
Gertie said Gus made the best fish fry anyway.

One evening, Gus couldn't find even one tiny
fish left to cook.

Soon Gertie came home wearing a new outfit.
"Everybody liked your fish so well," she said.
"that I sold them all. But wait until you see my
surprise for you."

It was a beautiful new fishing boat!
"The change will do you good," said Gertie, smiling.
"Now you can row far out and catch
still more fish."
"All right then," sighed Gus.

It was true.
With his new fishing boat, Gus brought in many
buckets of fine fish every day. And Gertie's
business was so good that she opened
a little fish store.

Gertie and Gus happily ate fish for dinner every evening.

MONDAY
fried fish

TUESDAY
fish stew

WEDNESDAY
broiled fish

THURSDAY
sautéed fish

FRIDAY
boiled fish

SATURDAY
fish soup

SUNDAY
baked
fish filets

And Gertie was making so much money that soon she opened
a fancy new store and had an elegant villa built
for herself and Gus.

Gertie also hired a French cook to prepare
their fish dinners and a French maid to serve them.

Gus didn't complain, even when Gertie made him
take bubble baths. But one day—instead of his
favorite fish—there was chicken with rice for dinner.
The next night, it was steak in a grape sauce.
And then, liver paté in a crunchy crust.

"The change will do you good,"
said Gertie with a smile.
"And speaking of changes,
wait till you see
what I have for you."

Gertie's surprise was a splendid captain's hat
and shiny epaulets,

plus five more fishing boats!
And five fishermen to catch still more fish.
Gus was now the captain of a fishing fleet.

As captain, Gus no longer had time to fish himself. Of course, there were mountains of whitefish, bluefish, grayfish, greenfish, big fish and small fish caught daily. And Gus could pick any fish he wanted and tell the cook exactly how he would like it for dinner.

But one day, Gus did not come home for dinner.
His splendid captain's hat hung in the hall,
also his gold epaulets. And on the table was a letter.

dear Gertie:
I'm leaving because
I like to fish for my
own fish.
It's more fun and
tastes much better.
sincerely yours,
Gus

"I can't understand Gus," Gertie said to herself.
"Being captain must be lots of fun.
The change will do *me* good!"

It wasn't true.
Working at the dock and selling fish every day
made Gertie's feet hurt more and more.

At night, Gertie felt so tired that she couldn't
eat her elegant dinner. And something was missing.

Meanwhile, back at their old cottage, Gus
happily went fishing with his old rod.
Still, even his favorite fried fish filet didn't taste
as good as it once did. Something was missing.
One night, there was a knock at the door . . .

It was Gertie.

"Hello, Gus," she said. "I missed you.
I understand now—catching more and more fish
makes one tired, not happy."

At once, Gus knew something, too. Eating his fish all
by himself made him lonely, not happy either.

How true! In their old home, they were both happy again.
And their fish dinners tasted just delicious!
Then, one evening, Gertie said to Gus,
"I have a big surprise for you."

And it was! Gertie had sold their elegant villa to the five
fishermen, who had turned it into an elegant fish restaurant.
Gertie and Gus were served a fine dinner, indeed.
"Our own fish at home still tastes best," whispered Gertie
with a smile. "But sometimes a change will do both of us good."

And it did!

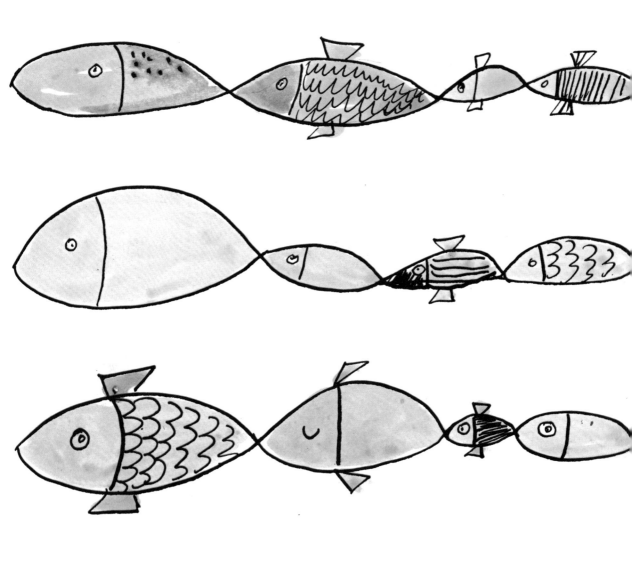